Claire: A Mormon Girl
Book II: Claire in Nauvoo

by Paris Anderson

cover and illustrations
by Velva Campbell

A Precious Child Publication
1356 East Oak Crest Lane
Provo, Utah 84604

ISBN 1-56684-053-8

Table of Contents:

Claire: A Mormon Girl

Book II: Claire in Nauvoo

Prologue

THIS is a story about Claire Nicol. She was born in Lanark County in Upper Canada (now called Ontario). Her mother was French Canadian and her father was Scottish. He worked for a newspaper there called *The Lanark Star*.

Claire had a twin sister named Marie who died from scarlet fever when they were eight years old. The whole Nicol family was terribly sad when Marie passed away. Not even the birth of Jacques, a new baby brother, could lift their depression.

One day, when Claire was eleven years old, Mr. Nicol was setting type for the newspaper, and he noticed a report that announced a series of sermons to be given by missionaries of a new religion called The Church of Jesus Christ of Latter-day Saints. When he went home for dinner that evening, Mr. Nicol told Claire and her mother about the report. Claire got very excited, but her mother wanted nothing to do with any "new" religion.

So Claire and her father went to the sermon alone, and when they returned, they were even more excited than when they had left. Mr. Nicol was at the point of tears as he tried to explain to his wife what the missionaries of this new religion had taught.

"And the best part," he said, "was when the missionaries talked about families. They said when their new temple is finished, families can go there and be sealed to each other. That means when we go to Heaven, Marie will be waiting for us!"

"Let's go find those missionaries," Mrs. Nicol said quickly, throwing her coat on. "I want to hear their sermon."

Though it was almost midnight, the family ran to the house where the missionaries were staying

8

and woke them up. Mrs. Nicol insisted that they give the whole sermon again. She was very impressed with the teachings, and the whole family was baptized a month later.

In the fall of 1842, just after Claire's twelfth birthday, Mama found out she was going to have another baby, and Papa decided that it was time for the family to gather with the Saints in a city called Nauvoo, Illinois, which stood on the eastern bank of the Mississippi River. That winter Papa sold everything they had, and in the early spring they set out.

In those days it was expensive to travel great distances, and when the family arrived in Nauvoo they were almost destitute. With the little money they had left, Papa bought a small piece of land in Nauvoo and rented a tiny cabin in a village called Zarahemla a mile from the western bank of the Mississippi.

That summer a new baby brother named Clairence was born. Claire's mother was soon able to leave her bed and began to work as a seamstress. Papa was able to spend more time working at a newspaper in Nauvoo, so the family's financial situation slowly began to improve.

In the early spring, the family moved back over the river to Nauvoo. They pitched in together and, with the help of good neighbors, were able to build a comfortable brick house.

This book, which is the second in a series of five, takes place in the summer of 1844 and is the story of how Claire learned not to be afraid of people who seem different.

Other important characters in this story are:

John Taylor--the new editor-in-chief at the newspaper where Brother Nicol works.

Sister Emma Smith--wife of Joseph Smith.

Joseph Smith--Prophet and first President of The Church of Jesus Christ of Latter-day Saints.

Sister Jane Manning--Claire's new supervisor at the Mansion House.

Sylvester Manning--Jane Manning's son.

Grandmama--Jane Manning's mother.

Brother Jonathan Beck--Claire's piano teacher.

Widow Dunford--Another one of Claire's teachers.

Chapter One

CLAIRE stepped into the middle of the broad, dusty street and started toward the Mansion House. During the summer it was easier to walk in the middle of the street. Men with wagons and carts always drove near the sides, and their horses left piles of droppings. Walking in the middle where she wouldn't have to step around them was much easier.

I miss Jezebel, Claire thought, glancing at a fresh pile.

A lot had changed since her little brother, Clairence, had been born. When Clairence was six months old, during the winter, old Jezebel died. She got so feeble toward the end that only little Jacques could ride her, and he had to ride without a saddle. Mama got sick that same winter. No one could identify the illness, but she became very sad and tired and had to stay in bed for almost two weeks. Sister Jones, a midwife in Zarahemla, thought the illness was due to a lack of sunlight and said the only thing they could do was wait until Spring.

The chief editor at *The Wasp*, Brother William Smith, quit working at the paper and went into politics. He was elected to the state legislature representing Nauvoo. A new chief editor, named John Taylor, was hired to replace him. He changed the name of the paper to *The Nauvoo Neighbor* and gave everyone a raise. Papa and

John Taylors Home & Printing office

John Taylor became best friends, and Papa had invited him to dinner twice when the family lived in Zarahemla. Both times John Taylor came with his wife and brought a smoked ham to give to Mama.

In the Spring the Nicol family moved across the river into Nauvoo. They lived in a tent until the big house was finished. Every spare moment that summer Claire, Papa and Mama spent laying brick, plastering walls and planing the hardwood floors to make them even.

The next winter the whole family enjoyed the cozy house. The wind couldn't blow through the brick walls, and no one got sick. The big house had large windows, so Mama didn't get sad and tired that winter.

Claire turned right at the next corner. She could see the Mansion House ahead, but it was still about a half mile away. Only eight buildings stood at the sides of the road before it. There was a wagon unloading supplies at one of the buildings. Claire started to run at a gentle pace.

By the time she arrived at the Mansion House she was perspiring lightly. A small bead of sweat trickled down her cheek in front of one ear. There was a small boy playing with marbles at the side of the house. Something odd about him made Claire stop and stare.

His hair had tight curly locks that looked like large buttons. His back was turned toward Claire, but occasionally he reached out to pick up a marble, and she saw his hands. They were almost as black as Jezebel's hide, except for the finger-nails, which were a milky pink like her own.

The Fox and the Sauk Indians used to live around here, Claire thought, feeling confused. *But Indians have brown skin, so that boy can't be an Indian. I wonder what kind of people have black skin?*

While Claire was staring, the front door opened.

"May I help you?" a woman's kind voice said.

Claire snapped her attention to the open door. A beautiful woman with soft, graceful eyes stood in the threshold.

"My name is Claire Nicol. John Taylor told my father that a girl was needed here to help with the wash once a week. He suggested that I come to help."

"So you're Claire Nicol," the woman said. Her voice was as sweet and gentle as a three-month-old baby's. "You're even more lovely than John said you were. I hope you're as clever as he said."

Claire blushed.

"Thank you, Ma'am," she said. "But I'm really not very pretty or clever. What is your name, Ma'am?"

"My name is Emma Smith, but you can call me Sister Emma."

"Pleased to meet you, Ma'am." Claire bowed her head like Papa did when he met a fine lady.

"And this is Sylvester. . .." Sister Emma motioned toward the boy with the marbles. "Sylvester?"

The boy didn't respond.

"For heaven sakes," she said, "sometimes I think that boy lives in a different world than we do."

Sister Emma stepped off the porch and went to the boy. She touched him on the shoulder.

"Sylvester, this is Claire. She'll be working here on Wednesdays."

The boy smiled and waved. It was a brilliant smile with the whitest teeth Claire had ever seen. The boy turned his attention back to his marbles.

Sister Emma started back to the house.

"You'll be working with Sister Manning. Sister Manning is in charge of cleaning the guests' rooms and washing clothing for them. Lately, we've been taking in more guests than usual, and the load is becoming overwhelming. I would like to help Sister Manning myself, but I'm so busy with the Relief Society that I simply don't have time."

They stepped into the house, and Sister Emma closed the door. The house was grand, full of delicate furniture and pretty wall hangings. There were several different rugs covering areas of the floor.

"This is a beautiful house!" Claire said.

"Thank you, but I would rather live in a shack," Sister Emma said. "This house is beautiful, but it's not a home. We have so many guests coming and going this place feels like a hotel."

"But why do you live here if you don't like it?" Claire asked.

"The Church needs a nice place where people investigating the Church, converts from the East and other important people can stay and forget about the cares of the world. Then, they can think about the Kingdom of Heaven more easily. It takes a lot of work to make this place look like Heaven. That's why Sister Manning needs your help."

"I'll do the very best I can," Claire said in a sober tone.

"Good, that's what Sister Manning needs."

Claire noticed a blond man with shattering blue eyes climbing the stairs gracefully and silently. He paused in mid-step and smiled in her direction. He winked. A flutter of warmth filled her heart as the man continued climbing and left her sight.

"That was Joseph Smith!" Claire said in an excited tone.

"That rascal," Sister Emma said good naturedly. "He should be working at the Red Brick store today."

Sister Emma laughed softly and shook her head.

"Anyway," Sister Emma continued, pointing to a white door with an oval window, "Sister Manning's in the kitchen. She's in charge of seeing to the wash, so you do exactly as she tells you."

"Yes, Ma'am."

Without hesitation Claire marched to the door, pushed it open and entered. No one was in sight, but Claire could see the back of a woman's dress just inside of the pantry door.

"I'm Claire Nicol," she announced. "I came to help with the wash."

"Thank heavens!" the woman said.

The woman came out of the pantry. She had the same color of skin as the boy out front. Her hair was tightly curled and pulled back into a bun. The darkness of the woman's skin was frightening to Claire, and she lowered her eyes.

"Are you Sister Manning?" she asked hesitantly, staring at the woman's waist, avoiding her eyes.

"Yes, but you can call me Jane."

"And you'll be my boss?"

"Yes."

"Well. . ." Claire said slowly, trying to think of an excuse to get out of the job.

"Haven't you ever seen a black person before?" Jane asked quickly.

"No, Ma'am, I'm from Canada. I don't remember any black people living in Canada."

"Well, don't be afraid," Jane said in a soothing tone. "Black skin is just the same as white skin."

Claire remained silent.

"I'll pay you eleven cents a week for helping me," Jane continued. "I know that's not much, but it's all I can afford."

"Eleven cents every week? That's more than I make sewing."

"Well, washing clothes is more work than sewing. Have you ever done wash before?"

"I help Mama do the wash at home."

"That's a good start," Jane said. "You see we simmer the clothes with lye soap in this tub here on the coal stove. Then we scrub them on the wash-board in the tub there."

"That's how Mama washes clothes."

"Good, since you already know what to do, take those buckets out to the well and get some fresh water."

"All right."

Claire took both buckets in one hand and started out the back door.

"Oh, and use that door to come in from now on," Jane said quickly. "The front door is for guests."

"All right."

Claire closed the door behind herself and started for the well.

Chapter Two

CLAIRE and Jacques were sitting on the floor by the fireplace reading a storybook when a crash in the pantry sounded and Clairence started wailing. Mama was sitting in a chair at the fireplace cooking dinner. She quickly pulled the pot out of the fire and stood up to see what was wrong.

She had hardly taken a step toward the pantry when Clairence came out with flour piled two inches high on top of his head and on his shoulders. His shirt was covered white. His face was bathed with the dust, except for a broad stream of tears on each cheek. He looked rather like the clowns Claire had seen in the circus back in Canada, and both she and Jacques laughed heartily.

"Did you spill the flour?" Mama asked the boy.

Clairence nodded and a cascade of white dust fell off his head. He started to wail again, and everyone laughed. Clairence screamed with fury.

"Calm down, Clairence," Mama said. "There's no need to get upset. The flour will wash off."

Mama crossed the room and picked him up. Clairence stopped crying as soon as he was in her arms.

"Claire, would you come clean the flour off the floor while I go outside to clean up Clairence?"

26

"Sure."

"Save as much of the flour as you can. We can't afford to waste it."

"All right, Mama."

Claire stood up, handing the storybook to Jacques, and went to the pantry. Mama carried Clairence out the back door.

The flour on the pantry floor was mostly in a large pile with two foot prints where Clairence had been standing. The keg he had dumped on himself was upside down in the corner. Claire righted it and began scooping with both hands and dumping the flour back in. The front door opened and heavy footsteps came in.

"Hello, Jacques," Papa's voice sounded. "Where is everyone?"

"I'm in here, Papa," Claire said loudly. "I'm cleaning up the flour Clairence knocked over. Mama's out back with Clairence."

"Calamity Clairence struck again, did he?" he said with a laugh. "He's the terror of all Nauvoo. What's for dinner?"

"Green beans with bacon, summer squash and corn bread with butter."

"And molasses!" Jacques yelled.

Claire heard the back door open and Mama's footsteps come in. Clairence's light footsteps came in after hers.

"Run upstairs and change your clothes, Honey," she said.

Claire heard tiny footsteps scamper toward the stairs. She dumped the last of the flour into the keg and set it back on the shelf. She picked up the mop in the corner and went to wet it at the well in back.

"Hello, Darling," Papa said to Mama as Claire came out of the pantry. "Will dinner be ready soon? I'm starving."

"It will be ready just as soon as we can sit down," Mama said. "Claire, would you take Jacques out and see that he washes up for dinner?"

"Just as soon as I mop the floor."

"That can wait until after dinner," Mama said in a sharp tone. "Your father is hungry."

"Yes, Mama."

She set the mop down in the corner and held out her hand. Jacques came running. They walked out of the door.

Jacques' hands and face were still wet when they came back in. His wet hair was neatly combed. Mama was scooping the green beans and squash onto a serving platter, and Papa was setting dishes on the table. Clairence was wearing a clean shirt and pants and was sitting quietly in a tall chair at the table.

"A terrible thing happened last night," Papa said.

He spoke in a shadowy tone that indicated this was an adult conversation and children's comments would be unwelcome. Without a word Claire took the silverware bowl off a shelf and began setting utensils at the sides of each plate.

"What happened?" Mama asked.

"The City Council declared *The Nauvoo Expositor* a public nuisance and ordered it to be removed without delay. The City Marshal took his five strongest deputies to their offices and completely destroyed the press with axes. They even scattered the type in the street and burned all the copies of the second issue."

"But that's wonderful! That was an evil newspaper published by anti-Mormons and apostates. How can you say its destruction was a terrible thing?"

"That's right, Papa," Claire added. "You said yourself the first issue was full of lies and slander, and its only purpose was to destroy the Church and get Joseph Smith killed."

"Aye, that I did."

"Besides, the anti-Mormon mobs in Missouri destroyed the printing press for *The Evening and Morning Star* in Independence," Mama said. "We're just doing to the anti-Mormons what they did to us."

"Aye, but the Mormons aren't a bloodthirsty mob. The Mormons are people who are trying to follow Jesus Christ and become like Him. We have to learn to treat our enemies with respect, charity and patience as Jesus Christ, Himself, would do. I predict grave consequences if we don't learn to love those that hate us."

Claire put the silverware bowl back on the shelf, then returned to the table and sat quietly between Jacques and Clairence. Papa said a prayer, thanking the Lord for the food and for the opportunity He had given the Saints to learn charity.

Mama stood and served the green beans and the squash. Claire served the corn bread and poured molasses on Jacques' piece.

"So, how was your first day working at the Mansion House, Claire?" Papa asked.

"It was a little frightening."

"Really? Why do you say that?"

"Well. . .." Claire put a fork full of green beans in her mouth and chewed. "There's a woman named Jane Manning working there who is really scary."

"Why does she scare you?" Sister Nicol asked.

"Well. . .she doesn't look like any other people I've met before. Her skin is black."

"Really," Mama said. "I've never seen a black person before. I've heard of them, but I've never seen one."

"And there was a black boy playing with marbles there. His name is Sylvester. They both seemed harmless enough, but they really scared me."

"Aye," Papa said, "people who seem different can be terrifying. That's why the mobs in Missouri persecuted the Saints. Mormons are different than most people living on the frontier, so we appeared threatening to them--just like this black woman appears threatening to you. The mobs in Missouri let the fear get out of control, though, and their fear consumed their hearts. My best advice to you would be to conquer your fear as quickly as possible. If you don't you will become more and more afraid until you become afraid of the fear itself. If that happens, the fear will consume your heart, and you will be lost."

"Your father's right, Claire," Sister Nicol said.

The family ate in silence. Only the clink of silverware could be heard until Jacques accidentally belched. Mama scolded him, saying only pigs and Scotsmen belched. Papa opened his mouth wide, then seemed to think better of the idea and continued eating in silence.

Chapter Three

CLAIRE walked past the Mansion House early Monday morning on her way to Brother Beck's lyceum. She pretended to be uninterested as she passed, but she peeked out of the corner of her eye to see if Sylvester was in the yard. He wasn't. Claire breathed an unexpected sigh of relief.

Wait a minute, she thought, shaking her head. *I don't want to be like that. I don't want to be afraid of people just because they're different. I don't want to be like the mobs in Missouri.*

She continued on her way, trying to think of a way to conquer the fear. Soon the problem became too confusing, and she turned her

34

thoughts to Brother Beck's lyceum.

Brother Beck sang in an opera in Boston when he was young, then taught music at a conservatory when his voice began to falter. Two years ago he joined the Church and made the trek to Nauvoo. On the way he stopped in Chicago to buy a piano and had it shipped to Nauvoo. He had been teaching piano in his home for almost a year. Claire had been going to his house three times a week for two months, but felt like an imbecile whenever she sat down to the piano.

Music just isn't easy for me, she thought, shaking her head. *It isn't like arithmetic or reading.*

She turned up the sidewalk to Brother Beck's front door. The silver haired gentleman was waiting and opened the door as soon as Claire raised her fist to knock.

"Good morning, Claire," he said in an aristocratic tone. "Come in and let's get started."

Claire led the way to the parlor and sat at the piano against the wall. Brother Beck slowly eased himself onto the bench at her side.

"Before we start, Claire, I would like to ask you some questions," Brother Beck said.

"All right."

"Why do you want to learn to play the piano?"

"My mother wants me to. She says I think too much like a Scotsman and not enough like a Frenchman."

"How do you mean?"

"Well, I'm really good at arithmetic and reading like my father is, and I can understand really well when he talks to me about things. He's a Scotsman and gets really proud when I think scientifically. My mother is French-Canadian, and I can hardly ever understand the things she talks about. She doesn't make any sense."

"What does she talk to you about that you don't understand?"

Claire bowed her head as if feeling a little shame.

"My clothes," she said hesitantly. "And my hair."

"What does she say about your clothes?"

"She says the colors don't go together, or that my dresses are dirty and wrinkled. She always says my hair is a mess and that I should spend more time brushing it and tying bows into it. That doesn't make sense. What does having a rag in your hair have to do with anything?"

"I see," the old man said slowly. He took a sheet of music off the stand on top of the piano and began to write numbers next to each note. "You think logically rather than aesthetically."

"I guess so."

"And your mother is hoping you will gain a greater sense of the aesthetic, if you learn to play the piano."

"I guess so. . .whatever that means."

The old man chuckled. It was a deep, rich sound. He finished writing the numbers on the sheet of music and set it back on top of the piano.

"Music probably doesn't make much sense to you, does it?"

"No, it sounds like noise."

"That's because you can't find any logic in the progression of notes. You see, music is really a complex mathematical puzzle. Each note has a value that can be expressed in numbers."

"Really?"

"Yes," the old man said, smiling widely. His teeth were very yellow. "Now, I've written down the value of each different note in this piece. I want you to go home and find the relationship between all the notes on this page and their values."

"All right," Claire said in an excited tone.

"And Wednesday, when you come back, we'll see if music makes more sense to you."

"All right, but I can't come back on Wednesday. I have to help with the wash up at the Mansion House on Wednesdays."

"All right, we'll change your lessons to Tuesdays, Thursdays and Saturdays."

"All right."

They both stood up from the bench. Claire took the sheet of music off the piano and hugged it to her chest. Brother Beck opened the front door.

"Good-bye until Thursday," he called after Claire.

"Good-bye."

Claire waved, then began skipping. She stopped as soon as she came to the road, looked again at the sheet of music, then walked toward Widow Dunford's lyceum around the corner and three houses down.

Widow Dunford was an old-time member. She joined the Church in New York nine years ago, only five years after it was organized.

Samuel Smith had brought a Book of Mormon to her house when her husband was out working in the field. When Brother Dunford came home for dinner, she showed him the book, and he stayed up all night reading. In the morning he announced they would sell the farm and everything they had and go live with the Mormons.

They lived in Kirtland, Ohio, then in Independence, Missouri, where Brother Dunford died of old age. When the mobs started to persecute the Saints in Independence, Widow Dunford moved to Far West, Missouri. Later, she moved to Nauvoo and set up one of the first lyceums taught by a Mormon.

Widow Dunford wasn't the best teacher Claire had ever had. She was so old her eyesight was beginning to fail, and she was stone deaf in one ear. She had a temper, like most other old widows, and some times she would hit the students with a switch if she couldn't hear what they were saying. On her first day at the lyceum Claire spoke shyly when asked a question.

Widow Dunford struck the back of her hands so hard one of her knuckles started to bleed.

Widow Dunford wasn't the nicest teacher, but Claire enjoyed the lyceum, anyway. Widow Dunford knew almost everything about the history and the geography of the world. She said when she was younger and her eyes were good, she had read every book ever written about European history. When she talked about kings, knights, armies and princesses, she got so excited it seemed like she had been there herself.

But best of all, there were times when Widow Dunford got tired and couldn't make out the letters on a page in a book. Then, she would ask Claire to teach, since she was older than most of the other students. That made Claire feel important. It was exciting to stand up in front of the class and help the other students sound out words. It was fun to see them get excited when they wrote their own names for the first time.

Claire turned up the path to the Widow's front door and knocked. There was a slight commotion inside, then presently, the Widow opened the door.

"You're tardy, Claire," the wrinkled old woman said. "We have a new pupil today, and I don't want my best pupil to set a bad example by arriving late."

"I'm sorry, Ma'am. It won't happen again."

"See that it doesn't. Now, go into the parlor and sit down. You'll have to sit in the chair in back. I told the new pupil to sit in your desk in front."

Claire walked into the parlor, curious to see the new pupil. She secretly hoped he would be handsome and about her own age. Then Claire could offer to help him with reading, and he would fall hopelessly in love with her.

Claire was surprised and a little disappointed to see Sylvester Manning sitting in her desk.

I can't help him with reading, she thought. *People would say rude things about me.*

Sylvester was wearing a sparkling white shirt and Sunday School britches. The shirt was very pretty against his black skin. His molasses-colored eyes were warm and friendly. Sylvester's forehead was full of folds of skin like a knotted rope, giving him a desperate appearance.

He must be scared, Claire thought and made her way to the back of the room.

She sat in the corner in a high-back chair Widow Dunford had placed in the back of the room. She could barely see one side of Sylvester's face from where she sat.

"Now, class, we're reading a poem by the famous poetess, Eliza R. Snow, entitled 'Oh My Father'," Widow Dunford said. "Sylvester, would you care to read?"

From where she sat Claire could see that Sylvester's face began to turn pale. It seemed as though his lower lip started to tremble. Sylvester abruptly dropped his face to his desk and buried it in his folded arms. He began to sob.

"I'll read," Claire said quickly.

She looked at the hand-written sheet of paper on the desk of the girl in front of her and began reading in a loud voice.

Chapter Four

THERE was an unfamiliar mood in the air when Claire walked to the Mansion House late Wednesday morning. The dark uncomfortable feeling was hardly noticeable when she first left her home. But when she was eight buildings away from the Mansion House, Claire saw two members of the Nauvoo Legion on horseback patrolling the street. They were dressed in full uniform and carried their rifles at the ready.

Claire smiled and waved as they passed. Only one of them waved back. Neither smiled.

When she was only two buildings from the Mansion House she saw other legion members putting manacles on a rough looking man and marching him toward the City Marshal's office. There were four more legionnaires standing as if to guard the Mansion House. Further up the road Claire could see a barricade across the street where legionnaires had stopped a wagon loaded with supplies. Two legionnaires were searching the wagon, and two others were talking to the driver. The driver was gesturing wildly with his hands. Claire tried to slip unnoticed to the kitchen door in back.

"Girl!" one of the standing guards yelled, "where are you going, and what is your business here?"

Claire stammered. She felt the blood rush from her face and her knees wobble. A few moments of uncomfortable silence passed.

"What's your name, girl?" another guard finally said.

"Claire Nicol."

"Do you work here?"

"Yes, sir. I help with the wash."

"Well, you better hurry, so you're not late."

Claire hurried to the kitchen door and knocked.

"Yes?" Jane's voice sounded.

"It's Claire, I've come to help with the wash."

"Oh, come in."

"Jane," Claire said after she had closed the door behind herself. "Have you been outside this morning?"

"Not yet, why?"

"Well, there are at least ten men with guns out there."

"Don't worry about that," Jane said, smiling brightly. "They're just here to watch the house and make sure ruffians don't bother anyone."

"Oh," Claire said, breathing much easier.

"Could you take this bucket out back and get some coal? We've got a lot of wash to do today."

Obediently, Claire carried the old wooden bucket out to the coal pile near the well and placed three large chunks in it. On top of these she lay several smaller chips. She came back lugging the heavy bucket, carrying it with both hands. She pushed the door open with her foot, then dropped the bucket on the floor. It made a loud thud. Jane turned to see.

"Lands, girl!" she exclaimed. "You're as strong as a man, carrying all that coal."

"Maybe I'm just as dumb as a man," Claire said laughing. "No one else would bother to carry this much coal."

She picked up the bucket again and carried it over to the stove. Opening the swinging door on

47

front with her foot, she shoved a chunk into the fire with both hands.

"Where are you from, Jane?" she asked, closing the door and dusting off her hands.

"I'm from Wilton, Connecticut. Where are you from?"

"I'm from Ontario, Canada. How did you get to Nauvoo?"

"We walked mostly." Jane brought a large basket full of white shirts over to the stove. "Now we just have to wait until the water gets hot."

Claire watched the tub for a moment, then dipped a finger in the water. It was only luke-warm.

"Did you join the Church in Connecticut?" she finally asked.

"Yes, I cleaned house once a week for a Presbyterian minister. One day a missionary named Charles Wandell came by the house and gave him a Book of Mormon. The minister threw it in the trash without even opening it. Well, I found it and took it home. The next day both Grandmama and Sylvester were sick, so I stayed home to take care of them. I read the Book of Mormon out loud, and when evening came we all just knew the book was true."

"That's grand."

"Well, Grandmama and I were baptized, and three months later we decided to come to Nauvoo with three other families from Wilton. We traveled with them as far as Buffalo, New York, where the other families boarded a steamer. But the Captain of the steamer hated black people and wouldn't let us on his ship."

"So what did you do?"

"Well, it was late October, and the weather was getting cold. We didn't know how far it was to Nauvoo, but we didn't want to go back to Connecticut because of the cold. So, we determined to walk the rest of the way. We walked until our shoes were worn out, and our feet cracked open and bled until you could see the whole print of our feet with blood on the ground. Sylvester cried and cried, but Grandmama never made a sound. We stopped and said a prayer to

God our Father, asking Him to heal our feet. Our prayers were answered almost immediately."

"That's wonderful! You must have tremendous faith."

"Yes, it's easy to have faith when you're different. If you're different the whole world hates you, so God the Father and Jesus Christ are the only ones who love you. It's easy to have faith when you know They love you and are your only friends."

"So, you think it is a blessing to be hated?"

"Yes," Jane said, then paused. "Some times it is."

Claire paused, thinking about the mobs in Missouri. Tiny bubbles began to form on the bottom of the tub.

"So then what happened?" she finally said. "What happened after your feet got better?"

"Well, after that we walked until we came to Peoria, Illinois. The City Marshal there arrested us and put us in jail for five days, because we couldn't show him any free-papers. Finally, Grandmama convinced him that we didn't need free-papers, because all three of us had been born free. He let us go, and we praised the Lord, singing hymns all the way to Nauvoo. A man named Orson Spencer heard us singing and took us in his wagon to this house.

"Sister Emma was so kind to us when we arrived. She fed us, bathed us and gave us new clothing and shoes. She asked us to stay here in the Mansion House and help her clean and take care of the guests. And when the Prophet came home that evening, no one had to tell me who he was. I just knew it. I saw him plain and I knew he was a Prophet of God."

"That's a wonderful story," Claire said. "Have you written it down?"

"I will someday."

The bubbles in the tub had become much larger and floated all the way up to the surface. Jane began dumping the shirts into the water. Claire picked a small wooden paddle up off the floor and began stirring.

"I saw your son, Sylvester, at Widow Dunford's lyceum Monday," Claire finally said. "He looked nice in that white shirt."

"I don't know what I'm going to do with that boy," Jane said in an exasperated tone.

"What do you mean?"

"He just doesn't like the lyceum or the Widow Dunford. Monday he came home crying and crying. He cried all day until bed time. He didn't even eat dinner. Yesterday, he screamed like the devil when I said it was time to go. He ran and hid under his bed and wouldn't come out. Today he sneaked out of the house when it was time to go, and I haven't seen him since."

"Really?" Claire said, as if surprised that someone might not like books and studies. "Why do you think he didn't like the lyceum?"

"He was embarrassed there. He's seven years old and can't read a word. He doesn't even know the letters. Grandmama tries to help him learn, but she can hardly read herself. I just don't know what to do with him."

Claire stopped stirring momentarily and stared at the shirts.

"I would teach him myself," Jane continued, "but I have to work at least fifteen hours a day to earn enough money to support Sylvester and Grandmama. I simply don't have time. And I don't earn enough to hire a private tutor. I just don't know what to do."

"Maybe I could teach him," Claire said hesitantly in a shy voice.

"Thank you, Claire, but I couldn't ask you to do that."

"It wouldn't be a bother. I'm already teaching my little brother, and one more student wouldn't hurt."

"But I can't afford to pay you. I can barely afford to pay Widow Dunford."

"That's all right," Claire said. "My little brother isn't paying either."

"That would be wonderful!"

Jane's eyes were very bright, and her smile was radiant against her dark lips. She dumped another wadded up shirt into the tub. Claire started stirring again.

Chapter Five

CLAIRE and Jacques had already eaten dinner and were sitting down by the fireplace for the reading lesson. Jacques was studying the drawing in a book of stories, waiting patiently. Clairence was sleeping on a blanket on the floor nearby. His hair was still wet from his bath. Mama was sitting at the table sewing. She was waiting for Papa to get home so they could eat together.

The sky outside was still light when Papa opened the front door and walked in, but a little darkness was beginning to set in.

"How's my family?" he said in a loud voice.

"Papa!" Jacques yelled. He jumped off the floor and ran toward his father with arms outstretched.

"SSShhh," Mama said with a finger in front of her lips. "Quiet, Jacques, you'll wake the baby."

Claire stood up and went over to hug Papa.

"And what calamity did Clairence cause today?" he asked.

"He found a mud puddle and took a bath," Mama said in an irritated tone. "Then, he filled his shirt tail and brought some mud home to share

with me."

Papa started laughing, and Mama got an angry look on her face.

"You wouldn't think it was so funny if you had to bathe him four times a day!" she said sharply in a loud voice.

Clairence began to rock his head back and forth on the blanket. He open his eyes and began to fuss.

"Mama," Jacques said in a delighted tone. "You woke up the baby!"

"Aye, laddie, that she did." Papa picked Clairence up off the floor and went over to the table.

Mama shook her head angrily. She got up, and took a skillet of beans out of the fire. She carried it over to the table and heaped two ladles full onto Papa's plate. She scooped one onto her own plate, then set the skillet down on a mat on the table. Papa was trying to cut the loaf of corn bread with one hand while Clairence was squirming and fussing in the other arm.

"Darling," he said, "would you please hold Clairence while I slice some corn bread?"

Without a word Mama took the knife and cut three thick crumbling slices from the loaf.

"Thank you, Dear."

"Papa," Claire said. Her voice sounded rather hesitant. "Do you remember telling me that I should find a way to conquer my fear of people who are different?"

"Aye, lassie, I remember."

"Well. . .." Claire cleared her throat. "I figured the best way for me to get over that fear would be to be of service to those people."

"That is very wise, lass."

Claire smiled as if proud of herself.

"Well. . .." She cleared her throat again. "Sylvester, that's Jane's son, he just started at Widow Dunford's lyceum, and he's having trouble because he can't read. So. . .I volunteered to teach him."

"What a wonderful thing to do, lass."

Claire smiled and breathed easier, obviously relieved.

"I invited them here this evening, so we can get started. They should be here in a little while."

"Here?" Mama said with a shocked tone in her voice. "You invited black people into my house?"

"Yes, Mama," Claire said in a weak voice. "I didn't think you'd mind."

"Well, I do. Now, you just march right over there and un-invite them. And next time you want to invite someone to my house ask my permission first!"

"But, Mama!"

"You heard me!"

"Yes, Mama. . .."

Claire started to stand.

"This is my house, too, Sister Nicol," Papa said. There was a stern edge in his voice. "Claire has devised a good plan. I'm not going to let you stand in her way. Besides, we have more important things to worry about now. Things are not going well in our city."

Mama pressed her lips firmly together and bowed her head slightly. Her face became red, and the muscles of her jaw became tight.

"What's not going well, Papa?" Claire asked.

"You may not have noticed, but the city is under Martial Law."

"What does that mean?"

"That means the city government is preparing for trouble. They've called out the Nauvoo Legion. The Legion is arresting suspicious characters and not allowing anyone to enter or leave the city without searching and questioning them first."

"Really?" Mama said.

"Aye," Papa said in a solemn tone. "I stayed late at the paper tonight talking to John Taylor. He told me he and his wife went to the Mansion House for dinner Sunday night. After dinner he and Joseph Smith went for a walk, and Joseph said, 'I have enjoyed God's safekeeping until my mission was fulfilled, but now that I have completed all that God required of me, I can claim no special protection.'"

"Really?" Mama said again. "And what do you think that might mean?"

Papa shook his head slowly.

"I am afraid to think of what that might mean."

There was a knock on the door. Claire got off the floor and went to answer.

On the doorstep stood Sylvester and a tiny old woman with black skin and gray hair. Sylvester's brow was knotted.

"Is this the Nicol house?" the old woman asked.

"Yes," Claire said, forcing a friendly smile. "And you must be Grandmama. . .or should I call you Sister Manning?"

"Grandmama will be fine."

Sheepishly, Claire extended a hand toward the old woman. She held her breath and closed her eyes as Grandmama took it. To her surprise Grandmama's hand felt just like her mother's hand.

"Well, let's get started," Claire said.

She led them to the fireplace where Jacques was sitting. Papa handed Clairence to Mama and brought his own chair over for Grandmama.

"I think you'll find this more comfortable," he said.

Grandmama smiled gratefully and sat. Her two front teeth were missing. Sylvester sat on the floor next to Jacques.

"Oh, I forgot," Claire said quickly. "This is my father, and that's my mother."

Papa shook the old woman's hand, and Mama waved and forced a smile.

"And these are my brothers, Clairence and Jacques."

"Hi," Jacques said and lifted a hand to wave.

Grandmama smiled and waved back.

"Now then," Claire said. She sat on the floor and picked up the slate near Jacques' feet. She drew a capital letter L. "This is an L," she said, "and it makes an 'L-L-L' sound."

"We already did this part," Jacques said.

"I know, but we're going to start over to see if you remember. Now, each of you draw an L next to the one I drew."

Jacques quickly drew an L, pronounced the sound, then handed the slate to Sylvester. He drew very carefully and deliberately, then handed the slate to Grandmama. She drew equally as carefully, then handed the slate back to Claire.

"That's very good!"

She erased the chalk lines, rubbing a rag on the slate and drew a new letter.

"Now this is an A. One of the sounds it makes is 'a-a-h.' If you put it together with two L's, it makes the word 'ALL.'"

Claire handed the slate to Jacques. He drew the word, pronounced it, then passed the slate on. Both Sylvester and Grandmama said the word very quietly.

"That's wonderful!" Claire said when she got the slate back. She erased it, then drew the letter B. "Now, this is a B, and it makes a b-b-buh sound. If you put it together with an A and two L's, it make the word 'BALL.'" She handed the slate to Jacques.

After two more letters, Claire read the book of stories, pointing out the A's, L's, B's, C's and D's. When she came to one she quizzed her students on the sounds of each letter and asked them to draw it. Grandmama giggled and smiled her toothless grin when she got one right. Sylvester laughed, too.

Chapter Six

BROTHER Beck was sick when Claire arrived at his house for her lesson. She knocked on the door, but there was no answer. She knocked again and heard a muffled sound inside.

Suddenly, Claire felt anxious as if something might be wrong. She pushed the door open a little and quietly slipped inside.

"Brother Beck?" she said in a loud voice. "Are you here?"

"I'm in the bedroom," a weak voice answered. "Who is there?"

"This is Claire." She went in the direction of the voice. "Are you all right?"

"I'm sick," Brother Beck said. "I haven't been able to get out of bed for two days."

Claire walked into the dark bedroom. Brother Beck was lying in bed with his eyes closed. He looked older than usual. Dark bands surrounded his eyes. His magnificent mane of white hair was tossed and unruly, looking rather like a white prairie fire.

"Are you hungry?"

"Very," the old man said. "I haven't eaten since I became ill."

Without a word Claire went to get breakfast for him. She came back into the bedroom in about twenty minutes with a plate full of cold ash-cake and fried eggs.

The old man was sitting upright in his bed, and his eyes were open. He was pushing his hair back with his gnarled fingers. Claire set the plate on the bed at his side. Brother Beck picked the fork up and began eating.

"What's wrong?" Claire asked. "You don't think it's the ague, do you? It's not the season for the ague."

"No, it's not the ague." Brother Beck said. "I'm very sensitive to the air. If there is trouble in the air, I feel the trouble inside of my body. When I was a young man in Boston, there was a hotel fire a few blocks from where I lived in which thirteen people were killed. I got so sick I almost died."

"There is trouble in the air," Claire said slowly. "Have you been outside and seen all the men with guns on the streets?"

"No, I haven't. I hardly go outside except to tend my garden and go to Church."

"Well, there are a lot of men in uniform marching in the streets and carrying guns. My father says they're members of the Nauvoo Legion, and they are searching and questioning people. They're even arresting some people. Jane Manning, a woman who works at the Mansion House, told me they were just here to protect us, but I don't know."

"To me it sounds like they're preparing for war," the old man said solemnly. "The things you describe sound just like the things I saw in the days before the war of 1812."

Claire shuddered inside.

"I hope not," she said. "War would be awful."

"Yes, it is awful. But, terrible things are possible. I've seen too many of them--children getting sick and dying, widows going hungry, old men with broken hearts. . .. That's why music is so important. It helps us celebrate the quiet moments and consoles us in our times of need."

"Speaking of widows," Claire said suddenly as if remembering. "I have to hurry to Widow Dunford's lyceum."

"Well, thank you for coming by," the old man said smiling graciously. "It brought a spark to my heart."

"You're welcome," Claire said, smiling herself. "I'll be back tonight to fix some dinner for you."

Claire hurried out of the house and ran to Widow Dunford's lyceum. She knocked on the door, hoping she wasn't too late.

In a moment the old woman pulled the door open.

"You're tardy again, Claire," Widow Dunford said. "If this behavior continues, I will have to ask you not to come anymore."

"I'm sorry, Ma'am."

She followed the widow into the parlor. Sylvester was sitting in her usual desk in the front row. His forehead was smooth.

Claire sat on the kitchen chair in the back. The widow stood at the front of the room and began lecturing about Africa. It was the second largest continent; only Asia was larger. Africa was the first continent to have its entire coastline known, but little was known about its interior. Claire wanted to listen, but there was something more compelling outside the window.

Ten legionnaires marched up the street toward the Mansion House. They came two abreast in five rows. Their feet lifted, then dropped at the same time, making a sound like horses walking on cobblestone. Gleaming bayonets were fixed to the ends of their rifles. Twenty feet behind them came another group of ten legionnaires marching in the same fashion. Twenty feet behind the second group came a team of horses pulling a cannon.

"Claire Nicol!" Widow Dunford's shrill voice said. "Are you paying attention?"

"No, Ma'am," Claire said in a shy voice. "I'm sorry, I got distracted."

"We were talking about Africa. That's the continent where Sylvester came from."

"He didn't come from Africa. He came from Connecticut. His mother told me. They walked all the way here."

The class burst into laughter.

"You weren't listening, Claire," Widow Dunford said sharply. "I was saying his ancestors were Africans, just like yours were Europeans."

"Oh," Claire said, turning bright red.

The class laughed again.

Claire bowed her head.

Widow Dunford continued lecturing, talking about the Portuguese explorers who risked their lives in search of a sea route to India around the tip of Africa.

Claire noticed a tight uncomfortable feeling in the pit of her stomach when she looked out of the window again. There was yet another group of soldiers marching at a rapid pace. In addition to rifles with bayonets, these men carried picks and shovels.

If she concentrated on the feeling, focusing all of her attention on it, Claire found she could make it grow. It grew quickly and seemed to blossom. Claire felt an urge to vomit. She raised her hand.

"Ma'am," she said in a quiet voice. "May I be excused? I don't feel well."

"Really? What's wrong?"

"I must have eaten something bad. I feel like I'm about to be sick."

"Well, I certainly don't want you to be sick here. You may be excused."

Claire hurried out of Widow Dunford's house, closing the door behind herself. She started to run towards home.

Not far past the Mansion House the men with picks and shovels were digging a trench in the road and piling the dirt high. Claire doubled her speed and didn't stop until she got home.

Mama was pulling weeds in the vegetable garden in front of the house when she got there. Clairence and Jacques were under a tree playing with marbles.

"Mama, do you know what's going on around here?" she asked in a quiet voice so the boys wouldn't hear.

"What do you mean?"

73

"I mean all the legionnaires around. Are they here to protect us from ruffians, or are they preparing for war?"

"I don't know. I suppose. . .."

Just then Papa rode up, charging on a dapple gray steed.

"Hi, Papa," Jacques said as Papa deftly swung out of the saddle. He started toward the house. His face was ash-gray.

"You two boys stay here while I go talk to your mother."

"Whose horse is that, Papa?" Claire asked.

"It's John Taylor's. He lent it to me so I could get home fast and get back."

Mama stood up and dusted off her hands and apron. Papa opened the front door.

"You come in too, Claire. I want you to hear this."

Claire followed her mother into the house and closed the door behind. They sat at the table with Papa.

"Terrible things are happening," Papa said. "John told me last night he and the twelve sat in council with Joseph Smith, and Joseph said, 'This is the loveliest place and the best people under heaven. Little do they know the trials that await them.'"

"Does that mean the Nauvoo Legion is preparing for war?" Claire asked.

"I'm afraid so, lass."

Papa paused for several moments and covered his face with his hands.

"I am afraid we will see the last of the Mormons to walk the earth," he finally said. "Apparently, God has abandoned us and will now allow our enemies to destroy us. I have been privy to reports of armies amassing in Warsaw and Carthage. Another army has already formed in Missouri. It is rumored they are already marching to Nauvoo."

"What shall we do?" Mama asked.

"There's nothing we can do. We can only hope that Governor Ford gets here quickly."

"Why?"

"This morning *The Nauvoo Neighbor* received an open letter from Governor Ford saying he is coming to Nauvoo to calm the situation. In the letter he promises Joseph Smith special protection and a fair trial if he is arrested for sending the Marshall to destroy the press at *The Expositor*. John Taylor thinks we should publish the letter as a special bulletin to help quiet the hysteria. He's setting the type alone, so I have to hurry back to help."

He kissed Mama and hugged Claire, then hurried out the door.

"You boys come in right now!" Mama yelled. "And don't go outside again unless I give you permission!"

"Yes, Mama," Jacques said. He picked up the marbles, took Clairence's hand and started toward the house.

Claire started out the door.

"Where on earth do you think you think you're going?"

"Brother Beck is sick, and I need to fix dinner for him," Claire said quickly.

"Well. . .all right. But hurry back. If there's going to be a war, I want my children at home where it's safe."

"All right," Claire yelled as she ran out the door.

Chapter Seven

CLAIRE made her way to the Mansion House late Wednesday morning. The trip took almost twice as long as usual. The Nauvoo Legion had turned the streets into a maze of trenches and dirt walls, and now the city looked like what Claire imagined the cities in the war chapters of the Book of Mormon must have looked like. The streets were so tricky that Brother Beck couldn't go more than a hundred feet from his house when he finally was up and walking. He had to ask Claire to go to the store to get some sugar and flour.

"My name is Claire Nicol," Claire said to the standing guards when she started toward the kitchen door of the Mansion House. "I help with the wash here on Wednesdays."

Two of guards appeared very nervous and alert, as if ready to fight. The other two had their heads bowed and seemed to be mumbling. One of the alert guards waved her on.

Claire knocked on the door and waited for Jane's response.

"Who is it?" a strange voice said.

"It's Claire Nicol. I've come to help with the wash."

"Please, come in," the voice said.

Claire pushed open the door. Grandmama was standing next to the stove, stirring a tub full of clothing. There was a very troubled look in her eyes.

"Where's Jane?" Claire asked.

"She's upstairs with Sister Emma. They're praying."

"Why? Is something wrong?"

"Haven't you heard?" the old woman said in a surprised tone. "Only an hour ago Joseph and

Hyrum Smith, John Taylor and Willard Richards were arrested and taken to a jail in Carthage."

Claire stood and stared, too stunned to breathe a word.

"If you want to help," Grandmama said, "the best thing you could do is go home and pray like Jane and Sister Emma are doing. I'll join them as soon as I finish these shirts."

Without a word Claire turned and ran out. The standing guards yelled something to her, but Claire didn't bother to stop and listen. One of them started after her, but she quickly left him behind. She didn't slow down until she was on the front porch of her house.

Claire threw the front door open and barged in. Papa, Mama, Jacques and Clairence were on their knees near the fireplace. Papa was praying out loud.

Claire stepped back outside to catch her breath, then quietly sneaked back in and knelt down next to Jacques.

Chapter Eight

ON the morning of June 29, 1844, Claire sat down at the kitchen table. The house was somber, even though Jacques and Clairence were up. They were in their bedroom playing quietly. Claire had already fixed a breakfast of ash-cake for them. She also fixed dinner for them last night. Mama and Papa hadn't left their bedroom since yesterday when Papa brought home the news of Joseph and Hyrum's deaths. Last night Papa and Mama had closed the door to their room and cried all night long. Even through the closed door, their sorrow and weeping could be heard.

"Papa and Mama sad?" Clairence had asked.

Claire told him they were, but couldn't bring herself to tell why. How could she? How could she explain to a two-year-old that the two best men since Jesus Christ were dead? How could she explain to a two-year-old that Papa's best friend, John Taylor, had been shot five times and was almost dead.

"They shot Hyrum in the face!" she whispered to herself.

She rose from the chair and started back toward the stairs. Her heart seemed to stir and speak to her.

Go, it seemed to say. *Go, you have important work today.*

"Brother Beck must need help," she muttered.

Without returning to her room to brush her hair, Claire trotted out of the house and down the road to Brother Beck's house. The streets were silent. People were all in their houses, and a deathly still seemed to blanket the whole city.

As Claire passed the Mansion House, she noticed the standing guards were gone. She felt her heart stir, telling her to go inside.

"But it's not Wednesday," she muttered and pressed on.

She was soon at Brother Beck's house, and walked to the front door. Beautiful and sad viola music was coming from inside. Claire pushed the door open.

"Are you all right, Brother Beck?"

"Yes, come in and sit down," the old man said without missing a note.

Claire walked very quietly into the parlor. Brother Beck was wearing a bathrobe, standing with his back toward Claire. The noble music he played was sad, sweet and slow, and each note seemed to bathe and comfort Claire's heart. Brother Beck never appeared quite as tall and majestic to Claire as he did at that moment. He played a long sweet final note, then took the bow from the strings.

After a moment of silence his shoulders slumped back to their usual position.

"I played that song for Joseph," the old man said, turning around. His eyes were red and swollen. "It was written by Nicolo Paganini."

"It was beautiful. I'm sure he would have liked to have heard it."

"Thank you," Brother Beck said. "I'm going to miss him. I never spoke to him at length, but ever since I heard his name I felt a yearning to be near him."

"I feel the same way," Claire said in a halting voice. She had never spoken about her feelings for Joseph Smith before, and found it to be very difficult. She cleared her throat.

"Yesterday, when Papa told me he and his brother had been murdered, I felt like my heart crashed to the floor and stayed there. I never met him, but I always thought he was my best friend. Now he's gone. Besides Papa, he was the only man I ever loved."

Claire felt her heart stir again.

Go! it seemed to say.

"I think, I better be going now," she said. "I just wanted to stop by to see if you needed any help."

"Thank you for thinking of me, Claire. Goodbye." The old man squared his shoulders, placed

84

the bow on the strings of his viola and began playing.

Claire closed the door behind herself. Again she felt an urge to go to the Mansion House, but resisted, reasoning that it wasn't Wednesday. She ran to Widow Dunford's lyceum.

The widow answered quickly when Claire knocked on the door. Her eyes weren't puffy and red as if she had been crying, but Claire could easily see a mixture of fear and rage in her expression.

"We aren't holding classes today, Claire," the widow said.

"I thought not. I just wanted to stop by to see if you needed any help."

"I'm fine," she said in a stern voice. "I always thought you were a sensible girl, Claire. But here you are running around when you should be at home mourning the deaths of Prophet and his brother. At the very least, you should be at home praying for John Taylor like everyone else in Nauvoo. He was shot five times, you know, and is about to die. It will take a miracle to save him."

"Yes, I know. My father told me."

"Then what are you doing here, girl? Go home and start praying for a miracle!"

Widow Dunford slammed the door in Claire's face. As she turned to go back home, Claire felt her heart stir again.

Go! it seemed to say. *You have more important work to do than to pray for a miracle.*

She stopped at the side of the road and lifted her hands in frustration.

"Go where?" she wondered out loud with some anger in her voice. "And what's this important work I'm suppose to do?"

Go! her heart seemed to say again.

"All right, I'll go!" she said in an angry voice. "I'll go *home!*"

Claire started marching home, her jaw tight with determination.

For once I try to follow the spirit, she thought, *and what happens? I end up on a wild goose chase. I might as well try to follow my nose.*

Beautiful music was coming from Brother Beck's house as Claire passed, and she stopped to listen. Her heart stirred again.

Go now! it seemed to say. *You have important work to do.*

"That's just my imagination," she muttered to herself and started toward home again.

The Mansion House was in sight, and for no particular reason, Claire crossed the street and walked to the kitchen door. She knocked quietly.

"Yes?" came Jane's voice from inside.

"It's Claire."

"Oh, Claire, I'm so happy you've come," Jane said. "Please, come in."

Claire pushed the door open and entered. Jane was sitting in a rocking chair near the door of the front room. Sylvester was on her lap. They both had tears on their faces. Claire could faintly hear an old woman's voice singing "Amazing Grace."

"My heart's been calling your name all day," Jane said. "Sister Emma asked me to wash this shirt, and I just can't bring myself to do it. I prayed to Heavenly Father, asking him to send an

87

angel to help me. He spoke to my heart and told me you are as brave as a lion and would help. Do you think you could wash it? The water's already hot."

"Certainly," Claire said. "Which shirt do you want me to wash?"

"That one in the basket." Jane pointed to a shirt with thick brown stains. "You'll have to scrub the shirt in cold water first. The stain will set in hot water."

Claire went over to the basket and picked up the shirt. It was almost completely covered with the stain. It felt heavy and stiff.

"But why do you want to wash this shirt?" she asked. "It's so dirty and stained it ought to be thrown away."

"Sister Emma wants to keep it in a chest with other tokens of the Prophet's life."

Claire looked more closely and counted eleven holes in the front and three in the back. Her hands started to shake and a lump grew in her throat.

"You go upstairs with Grandmama now and sing songs for Sister Emma and her children," Jane said and slid Sylvester off of her lap. "Claire and I have important work to do."

Claire dipped the shirt in cool water, rubbed it with lye soap, then scrubbed it vigorously on a wash-board. She dipped and scrubbed again, pretending the shirt was just like every other dirty shirt. After many, many minutes of scrubbing the stain began to lift, then disappeared almost completely.

Jane was standing at the stove with the wooden paddle in her hand. Claire put the shirt in the tub, and Jane began stirring. After a moment, she started to cry uncontrollably and had to set the paddle down.

"I'm sorry," Jane said between sobs. She sat down in the rocking chair. "I thought I could be strong like you, but. . .."

Jane covered her face with both hands. Claire took the paddle and began stirring.

"Don't worry, Jane," she said, trying to sound comforting. "I can finish this alone."

Jane continued to sob and cover her face. After a few minutes, Claire took the shirt out of the hot water, dipped it in cool water, then scrubbed with lye soap again. She rinsed the shirt twice, then ran it through the hand-turned wringer.

"When they told me Joseph had been murdered, I felt like my heart crashed to the floor and broke into splinters," Jane finally said. "He was the only man I ever loved, and now he's gone."

"That's exactly how I feel," Claire said. "In fact, I said almost those very same words this morning."

She spread the shirt out as well as she could, then carried it to the yard to dry in the sun. Jane walked with her. Together they hung the clean shirt on the thin hemp rope strung between two trees.

Jane's jaw was shaking uncontrollably and the streams of tears covered her cheeks. Claire noticed her hands were trembling and streams of tears bathed her own cheeks.

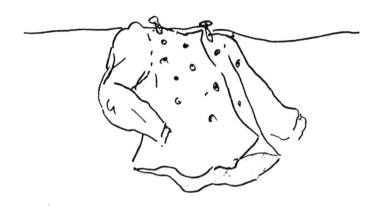

As soon as the shirt was clipped into placed, Claire reached out and hugged the black woman tightly, trying to comfort herself. Claire felt her heart stir again, but this time the feeling was warm and comfortable.

"Do you feel it?" Jane asked. Her voice sounded greatly relieved. "Do you feel the Spirit of Comfort?"

"I feel something," Claire said. "It makes me feel like I did when I hugged my twin sister before she died."

They held each other tighter for several minutes.

"I better get home now," Claire said when they parted.

"Thank you so much for coming by, Claire," Jane said. "You helped me more today than anyone ever has. Thank you."

"I'm glad I could help." Claire started toward home.

The walk home was much easier now. Several men with shovels were taking down the dirt walls and filling in the trenches in the streets. Claire arrived home before she knew it.

"Lassie!" Papa said loudly when she opened the front door. He and Mama were both sitting at the table. "I have wonderful news! God has given a miracle to our people. Only twenty minutes ago a runner came by our house and told us John Taylor sat up this morning and had a little stewed wheat and water for breakfast."

"That's wonderful!"

"Aye, and it's more than that. If God will still grant miracles to our people, it is obvious that He has not abandoned us."

"I have good news too, Papa," Claire said in a happy voice. "Do you remember that black woman I was afraid of because I thought she was different?"

"Aye."

"Today I found out that she's not different, after all. I hugged her, and she feels just like a sister."

"That's wonderful, lass," Papa said, standing up and walking to the front door. "I've got to go help fill in those trenches the Nauvoo Legion dug. I shouldn't be long."

"I'll go with you, Papa," Claire said and headed out the door after him.

"Don't be late for supper," Mama called.

"We won't be," Papa said and closed the door.